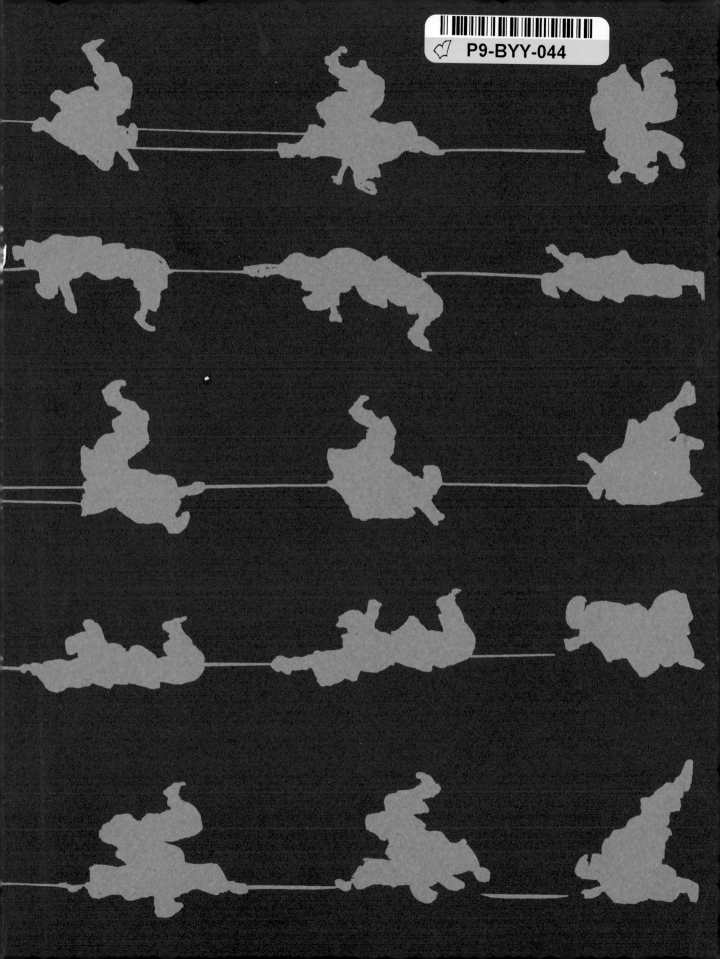

P9-BYY-044

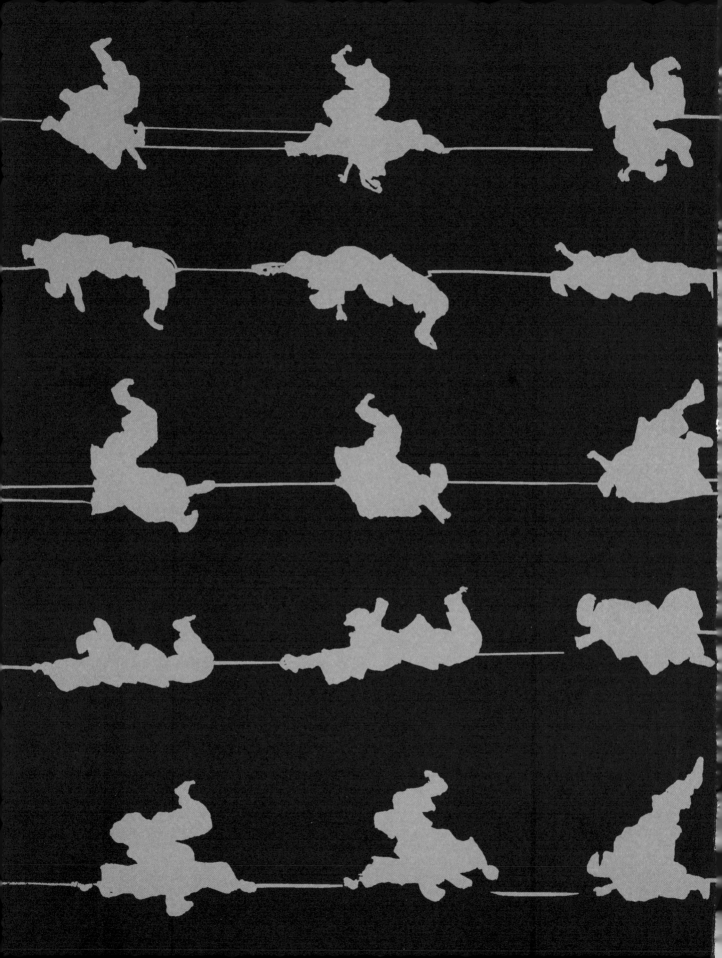

# nighttime ninja

By Barbara DaCosta ✦ Art by Ed Young

LITTLE, BROWN AND COMPANY
NEW YORK  BOSTON

ⓁⒷ

The clock struck midnight. . . .

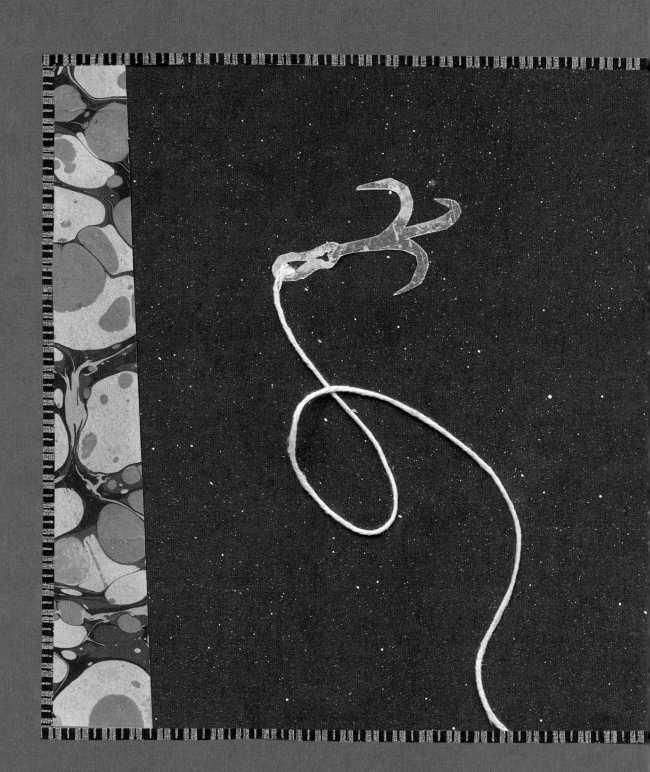

Hand over hand,

the ninja climbed and clambered.

Step by step,

he balanced and leapt.

The house
was silent.
Everyone
was asleep.

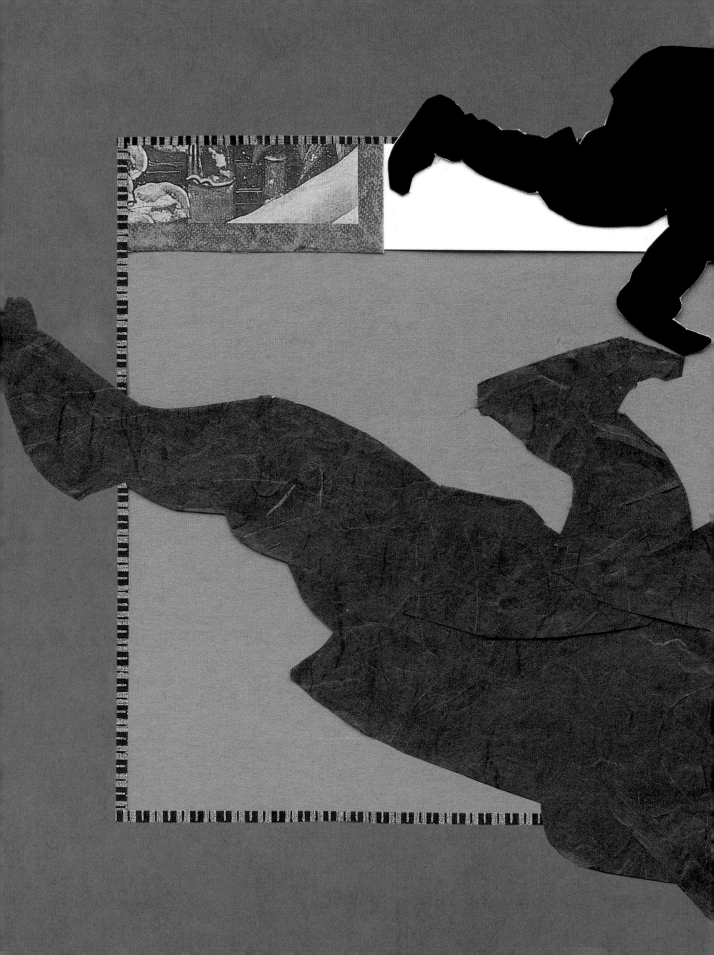

He crept down the
twisting moonlit hallway,

and knelt in the
dark shadows,
listening.

Wait—look!

He took out his tools

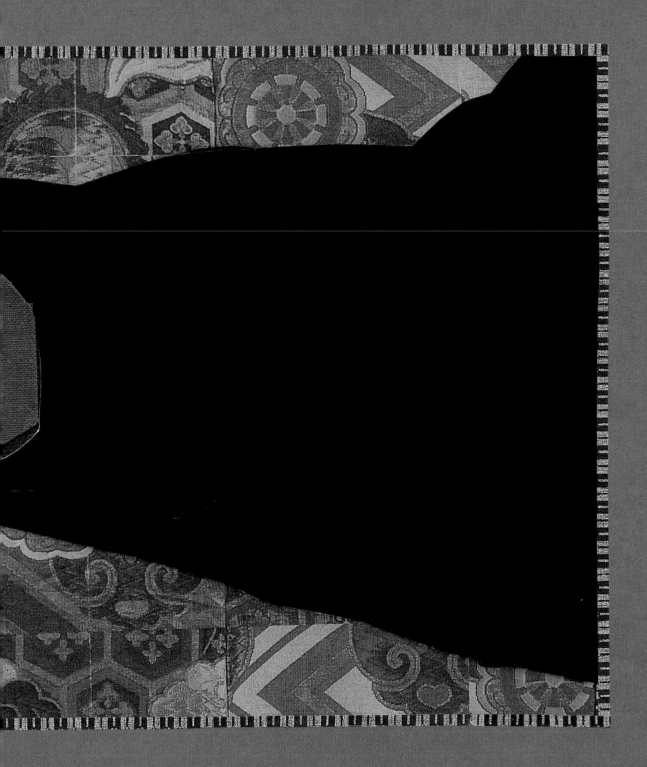

and went to work.

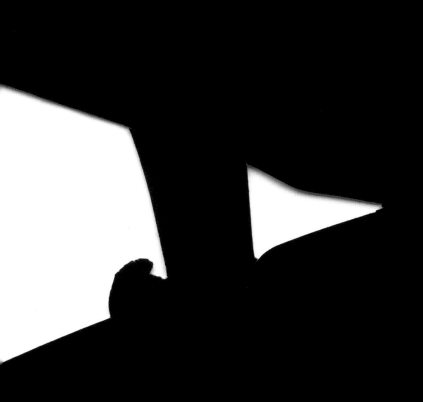

Suddenly, the lights flashed on!

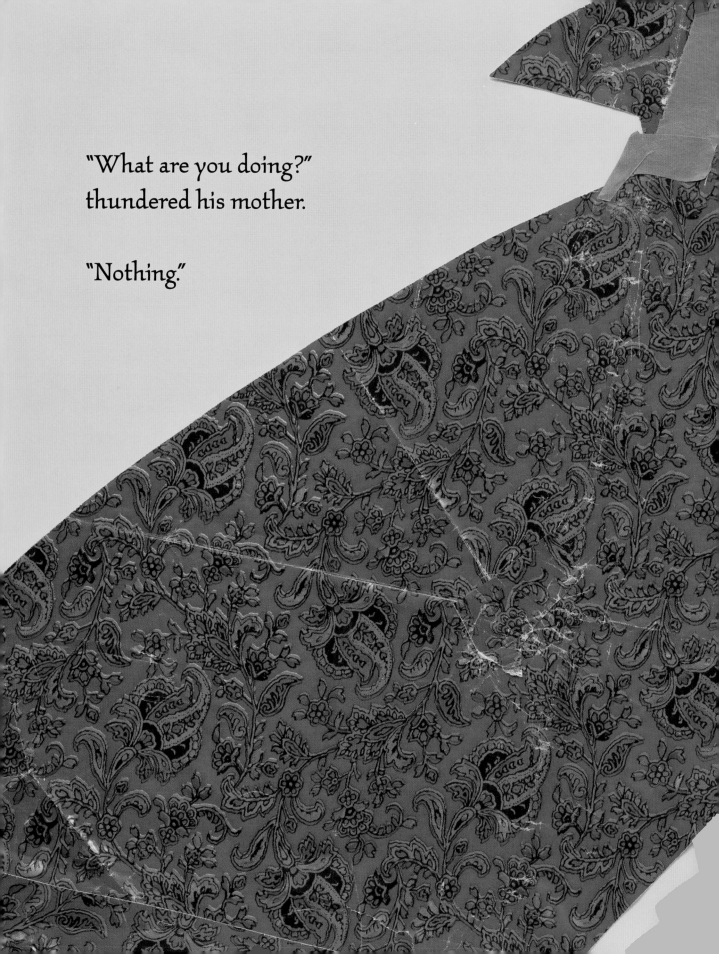

"What are you doing?"
thundered his mother.

"Nothing."

"Hand it over, mister."

"But I'm not done with my mission yet."

"Well, how about a getting-back-into-bed mission?"

"Sweet dreams,
Nighttime Ninja."

The illustrations for this book were done in cut paper, textured cloth, string, and colored pencil.
The text was set in Kallos, and the display type was hand-cut.

• Little, Brown and Company • Hachette Book Group • 237 Park Avenue, New York, NY 10017 • Visit our website at www.lb-kids.com • Little, Brown and Company is a division of Hachette Book Group, Inc. • The Little, Brown name and logo are trademarks of Hachette Book Group, Inc. • The publisher is not responsible for websites (or their content) that are not owned by the publisher. • First Edition: September 2012 • Library of Congress Cataloging-in-Publication Data • DaCosta, Barbara. • Nighttime Ninja / by Barbara DaCosta ; illustrated by Ed Young. — 1st ed. • p. cm. • Summary: "Late at night, when all is quiet and everyone is asleep, a ninja creeps silently through the house in search of treasure." — Provided by publisher. • ISBN 978-0-316-20384-5 (hardback) • [1. Ninja—Fiction. 2. Imagination—Fiction. 3. Bedtime—Fiction.] I. Young, Ed, ill. II. Title. • PZ7.D1218Nig 2012 • [E]—dc23 • 2012005492 • 10 9 8 7 6 5 4 3 2 1 • SC • Printed in China • Book design by Saho Fujii

*In memory of my mother:*
*the power of the mind, the warmth of the heart*
*—B.D.*


*To mystery, which holds our imagination hostage*
*in delight of its suspense and anticipation*
*—E.Y.*

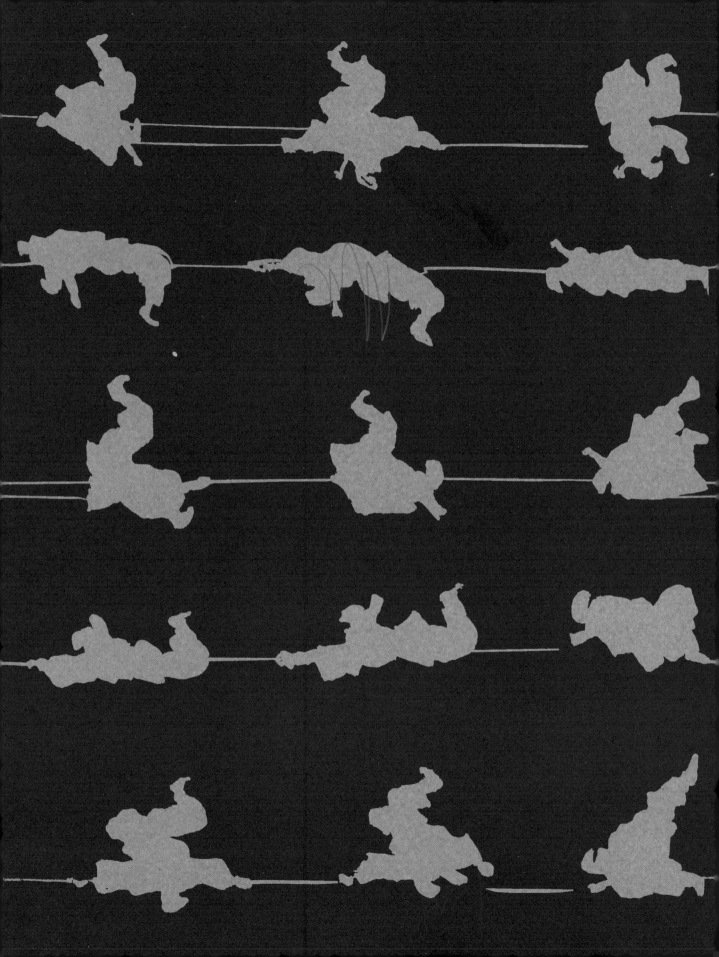